Granny's Dragon

Lisa McCourt

ILLUSTRATED BY Cyd Moore

DUTTON CHILDREN'S BOOKS

DUTTON CHILDREN'S BOOKS A division of Penguin Young Readers Group

Published by the Penguin Group · Penguin Group (USA) Inc., 375 Hudson Street, New York, New York 10014, U.S.A.
Penguin Group (Canada), 90 Eglinton Avenue East, Suite 700, Toronto, Ontario, Canada M4P 2Y3 (a division of Pearson Penguin
Canada Inc.) · Penguin Books Ltd, 80 Strand, London WC2R ORL, England · Penguin Ireland, 25 St Stephen's Green, Dublin 2, Ireland
(a division of Penguin Books Ltd) · Penguin Group (Australia), 250 Camberwell Road, Camberwell, Victoria 3124, Australia (a division of
Pearson Australia Group Pty Ltd) · Penguin Books India Pvt Ltd, 11 Community Centre, Panchsheel Park, New Delhi - 110 017, India · Penguin
Group (NZ), 67 Apollo Drive, Rosedale, North Shore 0632, New Zealand (a division of Pearson New Zealand Ltd) · Penguin Books (South
Africa) (Pty) Ltd, 24 Sturdee Avenue, Rosebank, Johannesburg 2196, South Africa
Penguin Books Ltd, Registered Offices: 80 Strand, London WC2R ORL, England

CIP data is available.

Published in the United States
by Dutton Children's Books,
a division of Penguin Young Readers Group
345 Hudson Street, New York, New York 10014
www.penguin.com/youngreaders

Designed by Irene Vandervoort

Manufactured in China
ISBN: 978-0-525-47463-0
Special Markets ISBN 978-0-525-42187-0 Not for Resale
1 3 5 7 9 10 8 6 4 2

This Imagination Library edition is published by Penguin Group (USA), a Pearson
company, exclusively for Dolly Parton's Imagination Library, a not-for-profit
program designed to inspire a love of reading and learning, sponsored in part by The
Dollywood Foundation. Penguin's trade editions of this work are available wherever
books are sold.

AFTER EXACTLY THREE DESSERTS and twelve stories, Granny said, "Time for bed! Let's get ready!"

"Okay, Granny," I said. "Only I better not go to bed, because I'm pretty sure there's a monster in my room."

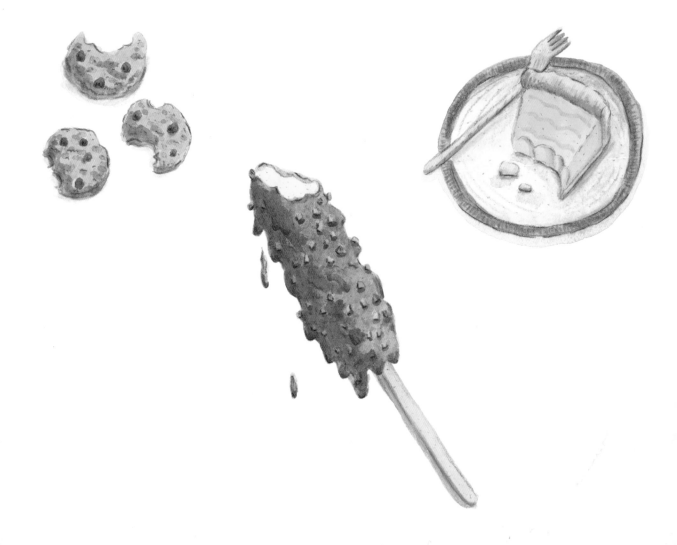

"If there is a monster in your room, he'll have to get ready, too," said Granny sternly. "He'll have to put on pajamas."

"Big scary monsters don't fit in pajamas, Granny. If he tried to put them on, he'd probably rip them all up with his huge, hairy arms and legs!"

"I will not let any monster that huge and hairy sleep in your room. He'll have to go out and sleep in the garage," said Granny.

"What if the monster comes back to my room to eat me after you go?" I asked Granny.

"Lucky for you, I happen to make a stew that is very delicious to monsters. I'll cook some up and leave it right outside your bedroom door. Then the monster will be full, and he won't need to eat you."

"Not even for dessert?"

"Good point," said Granny. "I'd better make him a monster dessert, too."

"Okay, **Granny**...but even if he doesn't eat me, the monster could still scare me with his big yellow teeth."

"**He**'ll have to brush his teeth, too. No one goes to bed around here with dirty teeth."

"He could growl at me. Or shake his arms in the air and say, 'Ooga booga booga booga!'"

"Ooga booga booga booga!" said Granny in her
scariest voice. "There. That wasn't so bad, was it?"

"No...but you're not a monster."
"I'd like to see your monster do a better job."

"Granny!" I said. "You have so much to learn about monsters. It's not just that they say scary things. They have special powers. Monsters can even GO INVISIBLE— so you don't see them, but they're still there—waiting to get you!"

"I see," said Granny. "Well, then, here's what I'll do.
I'll whistle for my very large but good-hearted dragon to
stay right by your bed all night and protect you. She can
go invisible, too, and she's way bigger and stronger than
any monster."

"How will I know the dragon is here?"

"How do you know the monster is here?" said Granny.

"I just think about him, and I know."

"So think about my dragon, too."

"Okay. What is she like?"

"She's powerful. Very, very powerful. One look into
her swirly green eyes, and even the scariest monsters
zoom away back to their monster worlds forever."

"Why are they so afraid of her?"

"Oh, they think she might growl at them. Or say, 'Ooga booga booga booga!' Or eat them."

"Would she?"

"Nah, she's a vegetarian. She does love my monster stew, though."

"And she'll stay right by my bed? All night long?"

"All night long."

I took Granny's dragon to my room. "Okay, Dragon.
Let's see what you can do."

"Everything's okay now, Granny!"

Granny shook her finger at the dragon. "Oh no, it's not! Come with me, Dragon."

"That's more like it."

"Good night, sweet girl.

"Good night, Dragon."